Among the greatest forms of human expression is the written word. Aneski's *Light Work* is literary artistry in poetic storytelling that invites us to adjust our sails as we explore the unpredictable and predictable depths of life, we'll all experience on this journey of self-discovery, self-love, and ultimtely self-discovery. Indeed, she is "Basquiat with a pen", painting with words. To all whose eyes it devours: Cheers!

~Lori D. Roberts Wiggins, award-winning journalist/communications strategist

"High vibrations for each creation was conceived by the divine. Adversity may find its way by design. It may exist but we resist cuz no weapon formed against a true prophet will persist."

From the moment Aneski (poet, performer, publisher, mother) opens her mouth, you can feel the power flooding out: in her voice, her presence, and her wise words, ringing across the space and enveloping every single person that hears them. The day the universe destined myself and Aneski to meet was a special one; we were both scheduled to perform as part of Tamara Payne's Dear Black Girl closing exhibition in 2023. Aneski would share the story of motherhood from a platform of divinity, her rhyme and rhythm further cementing her presence and might. After this moment, we would sing each other's praises, and I invited her to my monthly LightHouse Writer's Workshop series at Motor House.

Since then, Aneski has become a vibrant force and community member of the space, sharing her poetic genius, contributing sincere feedback to her peers, and adding an overall welcoming vibe to the space for writers of all ages and genres. Here, Aneski peels back the pages and allows the reader into some of the incredible works she crafted and workshopped in this space for all to see. In this collection, Aneski unflinchingly bears her soul on the page, sharing some of her most vulnerable journal entries, poems, and moments of gratitude for her artist community. These words will, without a doubt, become a timeless light bearer on your unfolding journey.

With Love,
Professor Unique Robinson
Baltimore, MD
Spring 2025

Light Work

By: Aneski Ana Kemsit

Printed by KDP
ISBN 979 -8-9879948-0-1

Book design by Aneski Ana Kemsit

First published 2025

DEDICATIONS

To my children:

Thank you for being loving and loyal to me. Each of you inspire me in a way words will never express. Each of you reflect some part of me. I am you. You are me. Together we are whole.

To TaeBird::

Thank you for being the anchor that kept me from drifting off into the horizon. Thank you for being the life raft when I was about to drown. Thank you for being that sturdy oar that propelled me across the sea.

To Professor Unique M. Robinson:

Thank you for being that solemn beacon on a solid rock not just for me, but to the whole community of writers. Thank you for the workshop, as it is a safe place in the center of chaos. There are literally not enough words to express my eternal gratitude for everything you do. May you continue to be blessed internally and externally, beyond the cosmic planes and beyond.

Table of Contents

MEET THE AUTHOR

Born as Thomasina Redmond, this enthusiastic writer published her first novella, Poison Ivy, in 2015, under her birth name; only to learn a few valuable lessons in the publishing industry. She immediately obligated herself to become a guide to other local authors, and founded 4Authors Authentic Urban Publishing Company, LLC. Being rebirthed under the pseudonym, Aneski Ana Kemsit, she set out on a relentless journey to be one of the most influential women in her hometown, Baltimore City.

Aneski is an author, writer, poet, publisher, producer, director, and emcee. Driven by her love for the arts, she has created several platforms to encourage and preserve the basic relationship between education and imagination. Having written and published her first poetry book, W.W.M.A.D What Would My Ancestors Do, in 2021, she then turned to hosting open mic shows, such as R.A.P. Rhythm and Poetry, Monday Madness, and recently Smackdown Saturdays, to create a network of performing artists and small business owners throughout the city.

As an aspiring stage performer and thespian, in 2022 Aneski decided to co-write, direct, and produce a play described as "...profoundly stirring, funny, (and) theatrically electrifying I Am Woke: A Poetrical Experience, featured a full cast of poets, and was received with demands, as well as an encore performance. Recently, she has become a member of the "Dear Black Girl" exhibit, curated by Art Professor Tamara Payne, where she recites an exclusive version of her popular poem, *"I Am God"*.

Through all of this, Aneski has also managed to maintain as Co-CEO of 4Authors Authentic Urban Publishing Company, LLC which has seven publications available online at Amazon.com, Kindle and other online marketplaces. Being featured many times on various media platforms, she can be seen on local podcasts such as Spitfire Poetry Shutdown with John Hansboro (WUBO), Blockboyz Radio (YouTube), and Muse Mondays with Shamise "Ladie" Jacobs (IG), where she consistently promotes her books including The Little Black Sheep Series, a children's book collection that focuses on learning the alphabet, numbers, and colors. Other books published by 4Authors Authentic Urban Publishing Company are ABC'S with Little Black Sheep and More by Aneski Ana Kemsit, God Won't Answer Me by C.L. DeLoatch and Blue the Love Bug by E. M. Wright.

Feeling compelled to form a community that promotes education, advocacy, and support for those that cope with what society has labeled as mental health concerns and/or learning barriers, she now hosts her own podcast, B'More Mind Full, with the intent to explore an array of topics that affect the mind, body, and soul. Also, to create a network of like-minded artists of all sorts of skills and trades and provide counsel in a safe and unbiased atmosphere.

A LETTER FROM THE AUTHOR

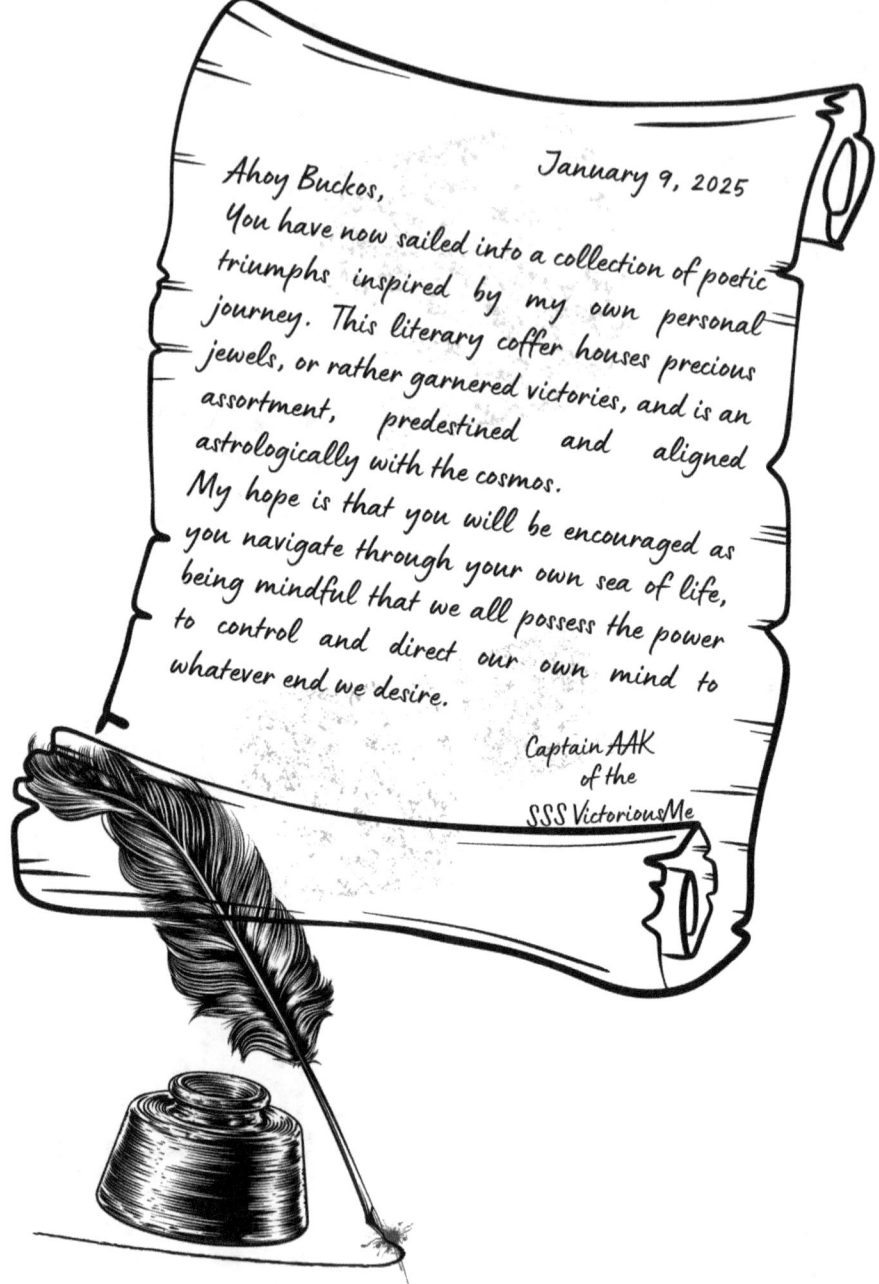

January 9, 2025

Ahoy Buckos,

You have now sailed into a collection of poetic triumphs inspired by my own personal journey. This literary coffer houses precious jewels, or rather garnered victories, and is an assortment, predestined and aligned astrologically with the cosmos.

My hope is that you will be encouraged as you navigate through your own sea of life, being mindful that we all possess the power to control and direct our own mind to whatever end we desire.

Captain AAK
of the
SSS VictoriousMe

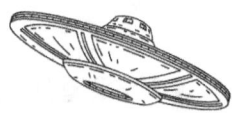

YOU oddly and ironically uplift me. Mentally and spiritually, YOU shape me; artistically assisting me in the mastering of my craft.

YOU help me maintain creatively.

YOU are as Unique as your name and I am so honored to have met YOU.

YOU and your partner are like glue. Yall have found your way into my heart and filled those tiny holes and it took for me to grab paper and pen to realize your contribution to me being whole.

16

Continued

And I hope YOU don't mind me being so bold, but the sun has returned after 365 days, making us another year old; at a time when getting ahead is our only goal.

Fate had her way and there is only so much gratitude I can show in one day, so I chose this day, tho I can never pay for your worth. I am completely honored to be blessed by your birth!

Yes, YOU!

YOU are Unique and Unique is your name.

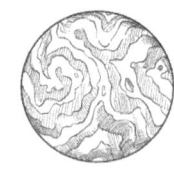

As we look back over our journey, may we realize destiny has been our common road

Dedicated to
Professor Unique Mical Robinson

Sink Or Swim

January 9, 2024

Well blow me down!

All six of us now live in my daughter's one bedroom apartment. I sleep on the floor, along my daughter's bedside, while everyone else is scattered throughout the small square footage, like shipmates amid a tiny vessel on the briny deep. Having been pirated by ill decisions and good intentions, somehow we have managed to stay a float, and not scuttle, but now we are dead in the water with what little duffle we could spare. We have been homeless for about three months. We have nothing but each other now.

Extravagant and Young

Prophecies
are infinite.
Like the
golden one,
we chosen ones
remain the one.
Our souls
don't die.
Our greatness
only multiplies
and our wisdom
is passed on
through
generations.

Our DNA stay
extravagant
and young
for our ancestors
are reborn
through every
living son.
So bow down
to the one
who puts it
in motion;
who commands
the waters
in the heavens
to fall like manna
and fill the ocean;

Photo: AneskiAnaKemsit

who raises
the sun
and sets it
at dusk til dawn;
who gives
the wind gust
to upthrust
the waves we
ride on.

High vibrations
for each creation
was conceived
by the divine.
Adversity may find
its' way by design.
It may exist
but we resist
cuz no weapon
formed against
a true prophet
will persist.

With promises legit,
Universal Laws
won't permit,
this our enemies
won't admit
cuz they hoping
that we quit.
Aht aht!
The fire's hot,
so we always
wear our
mitts.

For what's destined
is appointed,
and what's anointed
is protected.
Once the assignment
is accepted
revelations are
recollected;
a third eye opens,
as faith and hope
is resurrected.

Love and peace
fill the streets
of communities
from west to east.
We chanting proud
and worry free.

Catch us
"Xaydreaming"
or dream chasing,
either way,
we're so amazing!
We all win cuz
we're not racing.
We're embracing.

We are examples.
We are born leaders.
Come taste God's
sweetness,
here's a sample
for non-believers.
We bring good vibes
to the world,
besides it's
all a stage.
Like a supernova
our greatness
magnifies in
gamma rays.

We always
ready
to make
sumin shake.
We don't
delay.
And so many
blessings come
our way,
cuz we're gifted
from the
beginning,
being born
full of grace

A conception
by any mother,
has to be
heaven sent.
To birth a savior
like no other,
knowing only
nature is
immaculate.
Born with favor,
yet very humble.
obedient to
our Creator,
a physical
image of
our Maker,
full of Inner-G
and Inner peace.

We're in our
kingdom
for God is
in us and
we are
my brother's
keeper.

We don't fear
the grim reaper
cuz death can
not keep us.
We standin'
on bidness
with each
experience.
We are excellence
here on Earth.

We always
count our
blessings,
so we always
know our worth.

Prophecies are
are infinite
because
our souls
are linked
to one.
Many are called
but few
are chosen,
to be extravagant
and young.

Lor XayXay,

Photo:
AneskiAnaKemsit
This poem was inspired by
the album "X" and its creator
Lor XayXay. Can you find all
ten title tracks from the
album in the poem?

I Am Basquiat

October 19, 2024

My life is an unfinished
living artwork.
Poetically expressing
pain, darkness, truths...
purposed in my youth.
I am Basquiat with a pen.
Wielding words to shame men,
to expose our sins;
voices in my head,
vibrating high frequencies
absorbed by my dreads.

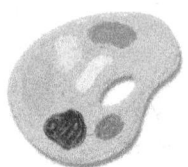

I too ran away from home.
City streets where I roamed
made for stories later told.
Long nights on park benches,
cold nights in vacant houses,
sheltered me from the harsh weather
but not from the harsh world.
Most nights I'd weep
not because I was alone,
but because my many personalities
clashed with who I was born to be,
and in reality those who look
at others like all hope is lost,
I've learned what they value is worthless
and what is really worth value
will never be purchased,
although it does cost.

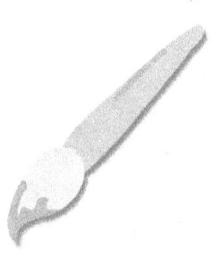

Forever will my heart belong to
those who accept my failures as
burdens of a creator who
bears a heavy cross.
I'm an emotional roller coaster ride
passionately described as
fine tuning my art;
creating poetry with every breath,
rhythmic cadences of my heart.

Basquiat painted with brushes.
I come to paint with words.
My stanzas are illustrations
like a colorful canto once heard.
Each pen stroke is a testimony
of my fiery existence in a cold world
and one day the world will pay
tribute to the beauty in my art.

I am Basquiat.
I am a poem on
an unfinished canvas
painted with pain,
darkness, and truth.
exposing sins with my pen,
purposed in my youth.

Dedicated to my nephew, Benjamin

Photo: AneskiAnaKemsit

Ship Of Shame

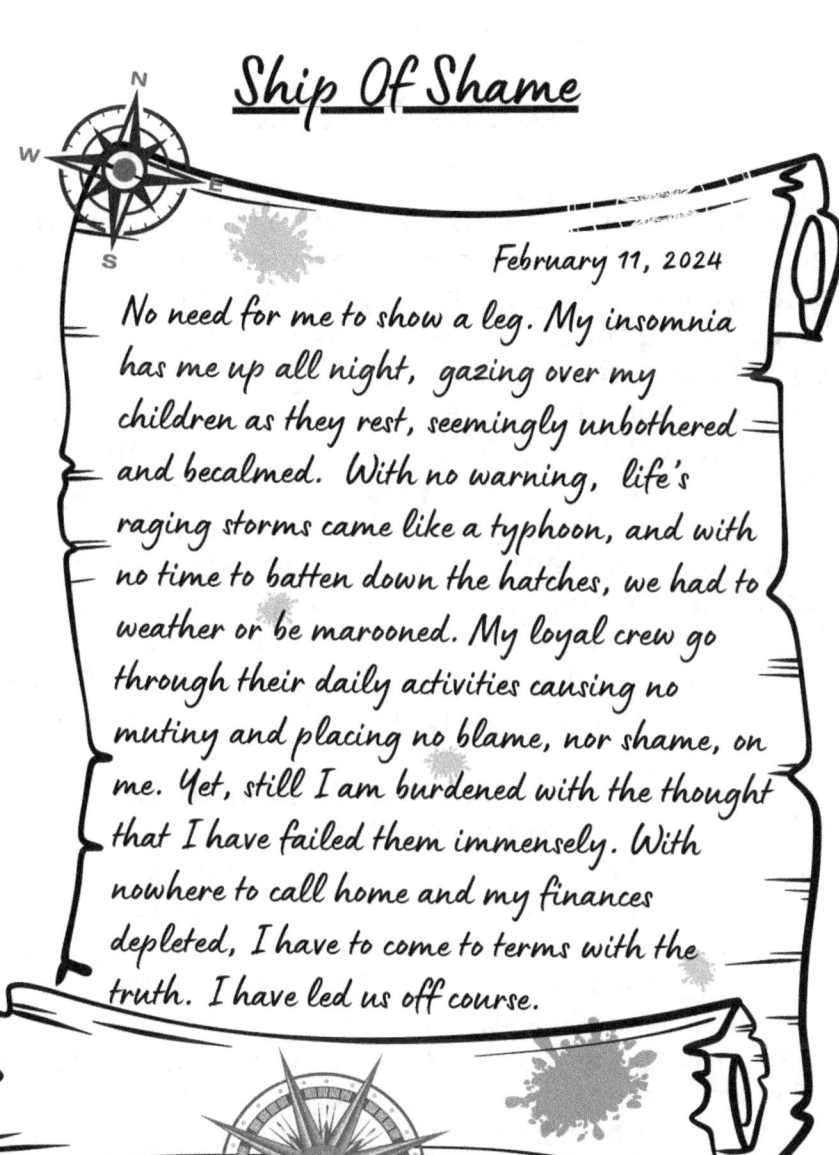

February 11, 2024

No need for me to show a leg. My insomnia has me up all night, gazing over my children as they rest, seemingly unbothered and becalmed. With no warning, life's raging storms came like a typhoon, and with no time to batten down the hatches, we had to weather or be marooned. My loyal crew go through their daily activities causing no mutiny and placing no blame, nor shame, on me. Yet, still I am burdened with the thought that I have failed them immensely. With nowhere to call home and my finances depleted, I have to come to terms with the truth. I have led us off course.

SNAIL STORY

The smoky, gray clouds seemed to shift in the opposite direction as I exited the bus. I was pleased to see the sky was clearing up, despite the faint smog that spat from the tail pipe of the bus as it was pulling off, with just a handful of passengers still onboard. I managed to fan for fresh air while simultaneously covering my mouth, in a display of rigid home training. After letting out a soft sigh and securing my backpack on my back, I began my daily trot to the place I often referred to as "the plantation".

It was really an Amazon distribution center, and it housed the ten-foot blue van I would use to transport packages through the city like a little blue obsessed, overworked elf. The vivid comparison seemed fitting for such a brisk morning although Christmas was well over four weeks away.

I didn't mind the weather at all. Being born in January, my body was already conditioned to such weather, therefore I enjoyed the cold, (especially on a morning like this). Not to mention the many past nights I laid across a bare bench in a park with only layers of tee shirts, hoodies, leggings, and sweatpants to comfort me as I settled in for the night. Back then, my hopes of finding shelter and food would have to wait until the sun came up. My days of being a homeless teenager were well behind me now, but periodically the memories seemed to find relevancy in my present life.

I pulled a fresh rolled blunt from my coat pocket and preceded to give it life with my handy, dandy *Bic* lighter. Just two flicks and a small flame gave my lungs such sweet satisfaction. I paused. I literally stopped walking, not even realizing I was caught up in a moment of bliss. I blew a heavy cloud and began to proceeded to my destination.

This was the best part of my little walk to the plantation. A shortcut through a winding trail, alongside a small stream on the backside of a neighborhood baseball field. I stopped at the bottom of the crumbling cement steps and blew out a bold puff. Step by step, my thoughts seemed to gleefully dance their way out of my head until they evaporated into the chalky blue sky. By the time my mind was empty of all that was, I had walked up the steps and reached the beginning of the trail.

One of the quirks of taking a hidden path is the opportunity to become one with your natural environment. I enjoy every moment enveloped in all of the simplicities of mother nature. From plant life, such as tall trees and large blades of grass, to huge geese and creepy crawlies of all kinds, Instantly, the short walk became a trail of self-reflection, honoring the intricacies of life. After a few strides of pure bliss, I was urged to look at the time only to see I had been dragging just a bit too much.

Putting some "pep" in my step and toting a short puff, (exhaling more carbon monoxide than actual smoke), I began to power walk the rest of the way, basically, so master could have his way with me. To help me focus on the task at hand, I decided to turn my attention away from the clouds above to the pebbled stoned concrete beneath my feet. After a few steps, my eyes caught a glimpse of something quite interesting.

Immediately, I came to a halt. I bent down as low as i could to see if my eyes were deceiving me. I leaned in and took one last light puff in honor of a moment of revelation.

"We as humans spend so much time hustling and bustling that we don't take the time to slow down and appreciate the little things," I thought to myself.

Lo and behold, aligned with my footsteps was a tiny snail, slowly slithering along, toting his home on his back. I fiddled in my pocket, pulled out my phone, and quickly snapped a pic. When I looked at the photo, I could do nothing but marvel at the divine. Then, my eyes caught the time in the top left-hand corner of my phone.

"Oh shit," I yelped.

Then I jogged the rest of the trail... so master could have his way with me.

This is Life.
You only learn by living.
-Aneski Ana Kemsit

Photo: AneskiAnaKemsit

Sick Of Sobbing

March 15, 2024

Shiver Me Timbers!

My eyes are swollen from a constant flow of heavy tears. I am a captain lost at sea. I feel like an ol' seadog fit to walk the plank. Although, I am now earning wages, time is still ticking and soon we will be up shit's creek. It has been three months and there is still no land in sight. I need to bring a spring upon her cable hard. I need to do a one eighty before the leasing office catches wind of us. I need to live up to the reputation that earned me respect from those who helped man this family from day one. I have wept long enough. It's time. All hands hoay!

Late Night Crazy Confessions

November 02, 2023

"Silence!"
That's what I
tell my brain
late at night,
all the way
into the wee hours
of the morning.
See, my thoughts
have been
bombarding me
and it's
almost morning.
I am tired
from thinking,
feeling like
an oxymoron,
yet words keep
rolling around
in my head,
like duck pins,
bowling.
I would diagnose
myself "schizo"
had not
my psychologist
already confirmed
I'm bipolar.

Which may explain
why my brain
fell like two
people at war
with themselves.
Segregated by
my emotions,
I still tell myself
I'm not crazy.
But maybe I'm
just on the brink
of being insane.
Simply because
I can't seem to
silence these
voices in
my brain.

Wondering.
Worrying.
Paralyzed physically
from a long day
on the job.
I'm working a
nine to five just
to come home
and be a mom.
Cooking and
cleaning through
the night only
to lay in bed
and be
someone's wife.

Love making.
First dating.
And now it's
time to rest,
but I can't
seem to sleep
with so many
unfinished thoughts
left to address.

Did I fold
the clothes?
Is the kitty litter changed?
Did the kids do
their homework?
Did the BGE get paid?
Too much to
be said,
not out loud,
but it's all
these conversations
going on
in my head.

"SHUT UP!"
I say silently.
"Today, you did
your best.
Yesterday is gone
and tomorrow
is not yet.
Settle down
for it is time
to rejuvenate."
I quietly tell myself.
"Don't say
another word.
Don't think
nothing else."

But there is
no cooperation.
I just fell asleep...
arguing with myself.

So Often Sore

Aye!   April 9, 2024

I finally have a vessel now, so I am able to travel at my convenience. As for housing, it seems too hard a task for even a landlubber to accomplish, nor a scallywag. These lily-livered banks won't bend, but I will keep lookin for prospects, although I work day and night. I ache from head to toe. I feel like I've been keelhauled as if I was rebellious teen.

Nevertheless, I won't allow myself to drown in the scurvy depths of depression, as I have had my fair share of near deaths and threats of visitin Davy Jones' Locker. The sands of time are runnin out and I dare not leave this task up to Lady Luck. My crew is depending on me, by hook or by crook, we won't be homeless much longer.

unbreakable heart

Photo: AneskiAnaKemslt

How many heartbreaks
does it take to break
the unbreakable?
I've contemplated
this equation
a thousand times and
still it waivers;
the query's labored,
mostly cuz the
only heartbreaks that really
count are only mine.

How many times have
I pleaded to God,
'cuz I felt like
I was dying?
With no witnesses around,
who can say
that I am lying,
when I felt my heart deflate,
it dropped me like
a paper weight.
And to think this was my fate
again and again and again.

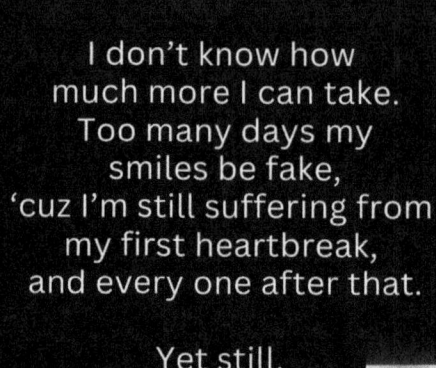

I don't know how
much more I can take.
Too many days my
smiles be fake,
'cuz I'm still suffering from
my first heartbreak,
and every one after that.

Yet still,
I need love.

Photo: AneskiAnaKemsit

35

Today: 1/26/21

I put a downpayment aka security
deposit on a house in N. Milton
Ave. This home will be the foundation
for elevation. Reestablishing morals
and values. Emphasizing obedience.
Encouraging Communication. These are
the things of focus that I must
discipline within myself first. The
children are in need of stability
and need to restore faith in me
as a leader. I can only show
where I have improved. Ensuring
them mental safety Emotional
Stability, & Spiritual security is
the main task. May all my
desires transpire so as above
and below.

                    Ace

Speaking Of Solutions

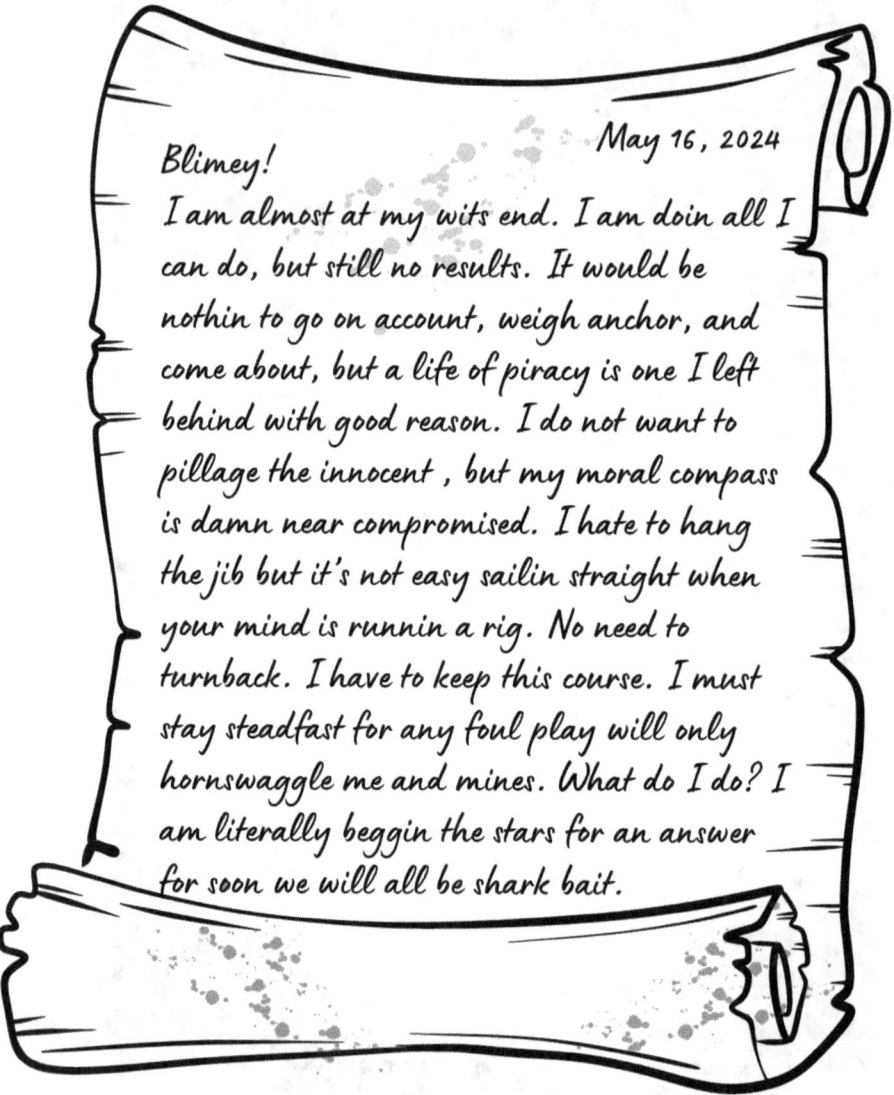

May 16, 2024

Blimey!
I am almost at my wits end. I am doin all I can do, but still no results. It would be nothin to go on account, weigh anchor, and come about, but a life of piracy is one I left behind with good reason. I do not want to pillage the innocent, but my moral compass is damn near compromised. I hate to hang the jib but it's not easy sailin straight when your mind is runnin a rig. No need to turnback. I have to keep this course. I must stay steadfast for any foul play will only hornswaggle me and mines. What do I do? I am literally beggin the stars for an answer for soon we will all be shark bait.

A Small Taste of Heaven

Had I known heaven
would open up its gates
and allow me to have
a small taste of forever,
I would have prepared
myself better.
Maybe with a
box of tissues to
pat my eyes dry,
cheeks stained as I cry,
despite every drop
being filled with joy.

For no gypsy nor
genie could have
given more freely
the magic bestowed.
This feeling of
being whole, completed
mind, body and soul.
All my fears erased
except the fear of
growing old and alone.
Which even soon is
eased by a soft touch,
a sentimental hug,
and a genuine smile.
I think I have fallen
in love for the
very last time.

Although last time
left me so desolate,
so close to death,
I vowed to never
love so hard or
give anyone else
all of myself.
And I didn't.
You forbid it.
Which makes it
much easier to
give all of myself
to you.

As, I receive all
you give to me.
Such is enough
to realize love is
so divine,
so destined,
so reciprocated,
So…mine.
Not just filled
with lust, but is
pure of heart.
If an apple falls
not far from
a tree, does
it's seed root
itself and still
give life a
fresh start?

Such should be
the same for
savoring love
and sanctity
over the bitter taste
of a broken heart.

Stars Of Salvation

June 27, 2024

Arr! I went from stargazing to studying the constellations. The sky is an astrological map, a guide through the spiritual, mental, and physical planes.

I recently met a few unique hearties in my travels on land, more time into that which is beyond the natural eye. They bellowed like the voice of Poseidon from beneath the sea. I was so unsure, yet still obeyed, and as a lost ship , along a dark shore, being guided by that distinct glow of a lighthouse...

I began to make my way to refuge..

LOVE at SUNRISE

I saw the sun rise today.
I batted my eyes and rubbed the
sleep away.
I heard a bird singing
and the wind whistling.
I heard a couple quarrel.
I heard them make up again.
I saw a heart shaped cloud.
I watched it float away.
I smelled the biscuits
my momma was baking.
She was always
mixing in the kitchen.
Sweet potato pies and
chocolate cake
to keep a smile on my face.
I went outside
so I can play.
Suddenly, I felt raindrops start
to fall from the sky above.
I hurried inside
and watched from the window.
After the serene shower,
I saw a rainbow.

.

I laughed as I chased
my lil sis
around the room.
I started pouting
when momma
choose me to
clean the bathroom.
I did what was
asked of me.
Then I sat with my dad
and we shouted at the TV.
I jumped like
the man holding
the basketball.
I ran and jumped.
I had a bad fall.
My dad kissed my knee
to comfort me.
He put bandages
on my wound.
and told me
not to cry.

It was now dinnertime.
Me and lil sis,
we ate and bathed.
Then we climbed
into bed.
It was the end
of the day.
I couldn't sleep.
My eyes were
opened wide.
I gazed at the stars
in the night sky.
I saw the man
in the moon.
And he saw me too.
I made a wish
and sent it
to heaven.
Soon momma and dad
tiptoed in.
They tucked me in tight as
they said,
"Goodnight, my love.
As this day ends,
let another begin."

Surviving Only Sustains

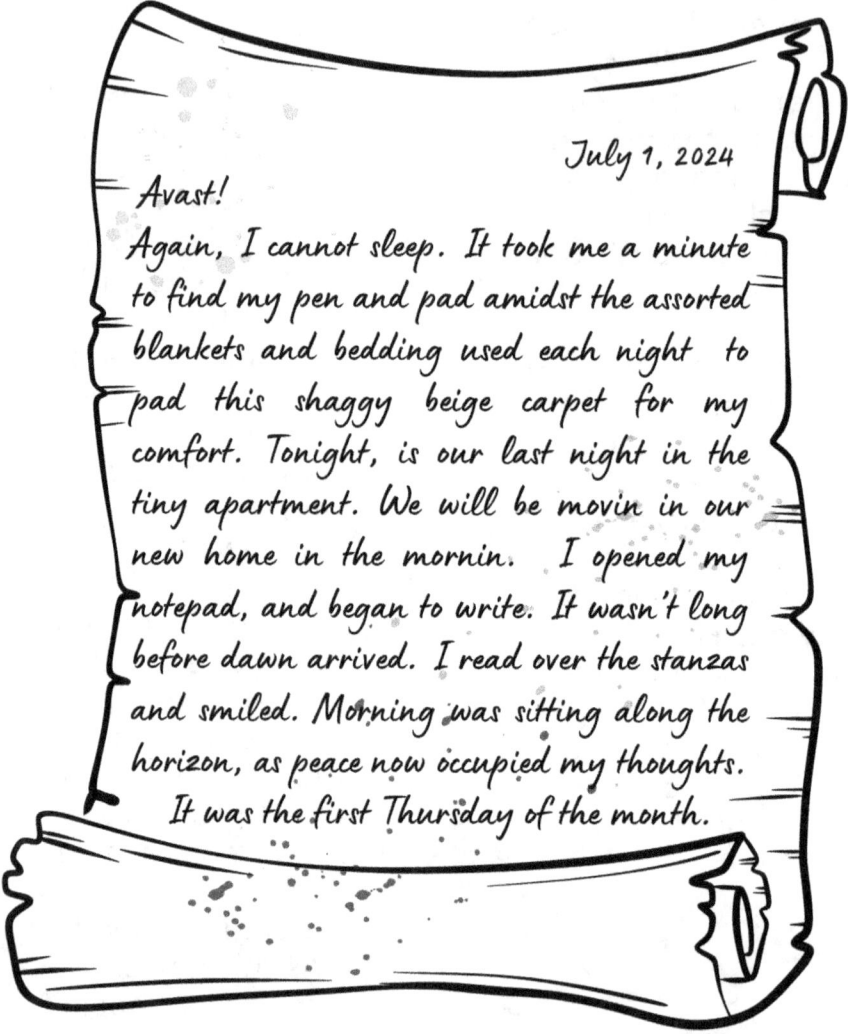

July 1, 2024

Avast!

Again, I cannot sleep. It took me a minute to find my pen and pad amidst the assorted blankets and bedding used each night to pad this shaggy beige carpet for my comfort. Tonight, is our last night in the tiny apartment. We will be movin in our new home in the mornin. I opened my notepad, and began to write. It wasn't long before dawn arrived. I read over the stanzas and smiled. Morning was sitting along the horizon, as peace now occupied my thoughts.

It was the first Thursday of the month.

stop da silence

POP, POP, POP
More gunshots are
heard.
Anova gun cocks,
more shots.
Now, I'm unnerved
as anova dead body
drops to da curb.
For some reason on
my block it's always
"Shot" o' clock"...
Man, dis absurd!
Police sirens soon heard;
flashin lights,
red, white, and blue.
Homicide arrives wit
CSI by dey side
collectin evidence,
but can't name a
suspect,
cuz dey ain't gotta clue.
Somebody seen sumthin,
but nobody knows
nuffin,
cuz bearin witness izza
job,
nobody wants to do.

So should I remain
silent as I watch his
momma cryin,
and his sons
and daughters tryin
to make sense of
what's insane.
And whats insane
is we constantly
puttin RIP in front
of
someone's sons
name;
followed by da
words
"Gone too soon".
Now we pointin
fingers
at da funeral,
placin blame,
and full of shame,
cuz anova father's
been
taken from his
family,
and now he's
gone too soon!

44

stop da silence

I don't think you hear
me,
so lemme cut
to da chase,
and get my point
across more clearly.
I pose dis one
question…
When does it stop?

Not just da violence,
but da silence,
da stagnation,
da miseducation,
da lack of dedication,
da unbelief.
When we gonna stop
allowin chaos to
take charge in dez streets.
Obviously dey have
declared war…
when we gonna
declare peace!

We deserve peace.
Our children deserve
so much better.
Dey deserve to ride
dere bikes up and down
da sidewalk without
dodgin stray bullets.
Hop scotch and pity pat,
ring around da Rosie;
not a ring of roses
around a memorial of
glass bottles and
dried up candle wax.
Dey say throw da
whole city away,
Naw… I say let's just
change our mindset.
It's no way dis is
meant to be da norm.

stop da silence

continued

I ain't callin for a truce.
I'm demandin dat it stops!
We killin each other,
den complain about da
cops.
I ask again my city,
I ask again...
when does it stop?
Not just da violence
But da silence.
So I need you to
make some noise
if you're tired.

RECONNECT

DECEMBER 07, 2023

I sat down
for a moment
to recollect.
At the end
of a long day,
I had to reconnect
Lately, I've been
feeling like I
was born with
a defect.
I keep trying to
find my nitch
but all I'm
finding is
I'm a reject.

Is it me?

I've been through
a lot and I'm
still going through,
and I figure it
will make sense,
if I look back
and see if I grew.
Besides, I am grown,
so I would think
I would know
what to do.

Now I'm at
this crossroad.
It's that fork
where no matter
which road
is took,
it will always lead
between a
rock and a
hard place.
Frankly, I'm tired
of being stuck
but it seems
I'm always there
so I call it
my space.
Because socially
I'm not really here.
I maneuver due
to the auto pilot
setting activated
by society.

And now I'm tired
and I've decided
to sit down
and reconnect
with self.
Lately, I've seemed
to put her on
the bottom shelf.

And maybe that
is why I
am feeling
all cluttered and
covered in dust.
I've forgotten to
show myself
some attention.
I've forgotten to
give back
to myself.
Instead, I have
spread myself so
thin, loving
everyone who
failed to receive
and reciprocate
the same need.

If I had to
rewrite my
mission statement,
the first line
would be:
I need me to
take care of me
and pour into
myself as if
I am the charity.

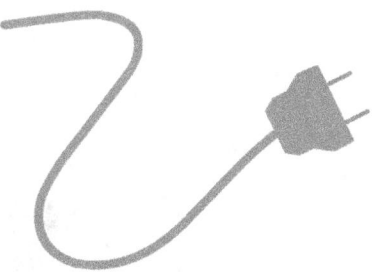

Then I can extend
a helping hand
without draining
my own battery.
Self-perseverance
is the preservation
of one's
own energy.
Giving to much
causes an
overload,
glitches,
short circuits
disrupting us
mentally.

This experience is
referred to as
a disconnect.
If this happens,
take a moment.,
sit down and
reconnect.

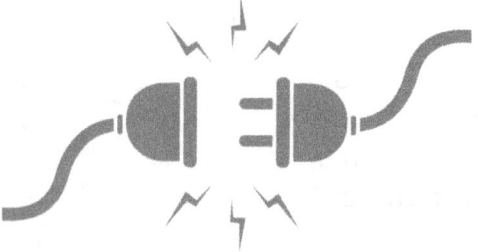

Fucked Up Wita Smile

I gotta
wear my
fucked up
wita smile.
Cuz deep inside
I'm so
fucked up
but from
da look on
my face
a nigga might
not kno how.
And if dey did,
(tah)
dey would
prolly cry.
But not I!
I hold my
head so high
a nigga
would think
fucked up
was a style.

I mean I'm
fucked up
like overdue
rent,
ducking repo
but payin
insurance.
All da while
prayin
to ensure
da lights
don't go out.

Ain't no food
in da fridge
cuz issa
drought in my
bank account,
late for work
cuz I need gas
and im low
on cash,
feed da meter
Or feed
my tummy;

Cashapp
da gas man
cuz my lungs
are hungry
and I need
to eat;
knees achin
from workin
dis back breakin
job all week.
I need a
chiropractor,
a massage
therapist,
an orthopedic,
or an all
in one,
cuz I've been
walkin for days,
workin hard,
and makin plays.

My IOU's
are waist deep
and mentally
I'm on da brink.
I stay on
da edge,
so I stay
wita drink,
cuz when I
get a minute
to sit back
and think;
I can't
breathe under
da suffocation
of offspring
dat seem to
have no regard
for people
who exist
outside
demselves.
Dey bombard
my mind,
I lose track
of time;
dat's why
I'm always
in a rush
and truth is
I'm really
just
fucked up!

I've been
fucked up
for a while.
But I'll
be damned
if I let
the world
know how
fucked up
I really am.
So Imma be
sure to
wear my
fucked up
glittered up
like its glam.
Imma
make over
my fucked up
until I forget
dat I am.
Imma rock my
fucked up
til it goes
outta style.
And it will…

But until den
Imma wear my
fucked up
wita smile.

51

FINAL THOUGHT

I am certain you were drawn to this book because you were in need of that empathetic feeling of being lost at sea and seeking that tiny beacon we call hope. I have faith you have found that very light which can lead you out of your dark place. In doing so I encourage you to journal your own thoughts to have as a reminder of your resilience.

May your S.O.S. bring your own Story of Success.

Sincerly
Aveski Ava Kemsit

www.ingramcontent.com/pod-product-compliance
Lightning Source LLC
Chambersburg PA
CBHW052144220626
47052CB00005B/1191